# The Hullabaloo Bugaboo Day

## Sheree Fitch

## illustrated by Jill Quinn

Pottersfield Press, Lawrencetown Beach
Nova Scotia, Canada

**Back cover photo by Paul Darrow**

**Canadian Cataloguing in Publication Data**

Fitch, Sheree
    The hullabaloo bugaboo day
    ISBN 1–895900–08–5
I. Quinn, Jill.        II. Title.
PS8561.I86H87 1997        jC813'.54        C97–950164–4
PZ7.F57Hu 1997

Pottersfield Press gratefully acknowledges the ongoing support of the Nova Scotia Department of Education, Cultural Affairs Division as well as the Canada Council, and the Department of Canadian Heritage.

Pottersfield Press
83 Leslie Road
East Lawrencetown
Nova Scotia B2Z 1P8
To order, phone 1-800-NIMBUS9

THE CANADA COUNCIL | LE CONSEIL DES ARTS
FOR THE ARTS | DU CANADA
SINCE 1957 | DEPUIS 1957

Printed in Canada

To my mother, my Aunt Stella, my cousin Wendy, and all secretaries who hold things together. And smile!

— S.F.


For Laurie Boucher, whose encouragement, inspiration and love helped to make this book possible.

— J.Q.

## Chapter 1
## The Way It Was

Upper Millidocket Elementary School was an exceptional school.

The teachers at Upper Millidocket Elementary School were exceptional teachers.

When they taught lessons their faces shone like the sun. Well, most days.

When they said, "Good morning class," their voices were smooth as maple syrup. Well, almost always.

The teachers loved each and every one of their students. Or so it usually seemed.

And best of all, those exceptional teachers never never never never NEVER gave homework. Well, almost never.

The students of Upper Millidocket Elementary School were exceptional too.

When they learned their lessons their eyes sparkled like stars. Really.

When they said, "Good morning, teacher," their voices were like angel songs. At least when they tried hard.

The students loved each and every one of their teachers.

And best of all, they always always always always ALWAYS did their homework. Well, almost always.

Mr. Tiggle was an exceptional principal.

"Wise as an owl," some said.

"Kind as a koala bear," said others.

"Smells like peppermints and cinnamon," said everyone in Primary.

Mr. Tiggle always stopped to tie up the laces of primary students when lacing up was needed.

Mr. Tiggle always had a silly poem to read over the intercom every morning because, he said, "A poem a day keeps the bugaboos away."

Bugaboo was Mr. Tiggle's silly word for trouble.

He liked silly words.

He liked cheerful words.

He liked words so much that every day he put up a new word on the bulletin board.

He called it Mr. Tiggle's Delicious Word List.

Whether it was first thing in the morning or last thing at night you could always count on Mr. Tiggle to say the same thing:

"Oh, what a wonderful Upper Millidocket Elementary School Day!"

And it always had been. And it always was.

Until the day Miss Argyle, the exceptional Upper Millidocket Elementary School secretary, disappeared.

## Chapter 2
## Where oh Where is Miss Argyle?

Here's how it started.

Mr. Tiggle rang the bell. Same as always.

He made the announcements. Same as always.

But, on this day, he forgot to say a poem.

At exactly 8:35 A.M., after the announcements, Miss Argyle left her desk. She walked down the hall to return a book to Mrs. Graves, the second grade teacher. As Miss Argyle was passing the broom closet, she heard a noise.

She opened the door.

She stepped inside.

A mouse scurried underneath her feet and into a hole in the wall.

Miss Argyle, who actually had a deep affection for mice, was startled.

She jumped.

She gave a small shriek, a kind of eek!!! sound, and the door slammed shut.

She was locked inside.

Ordinarily, Miss Argyle would have just pounded on that door. She would have just yelled for help.

But just as she was beginning to yell for help, Mr. Tiggle ran by the broom closet door saying: "Where oh where is Miss Argyle? I can't find her. Why, this whole school would fall apart without her!"

Now Miss Argyle had been feeling a little neglected lately. She had been doing a lot of work and no one was saying, "Good job, Miss Argyle." Even a thank you now and then would be nice, she thought. But everyone was so busy. Especially Miss Argyle. This is what she had been doing:

*Answering phones and delivering notices and taking messages and typing notices and getting Band-Aids and looking for lost boots and finding the right piece of paper and collecting lunch money and placing pizza orders and phoning parents and talking to parents and arranging a book fair and organizing a flea market and fixing the photocopy machine and copying enough for everyone and stapling things together and thumbtacking art work up in the halls and signing for deliveries and finding the Scotch tape and buying extra glue and retrieving basketballs when they bounced out of the gym and looking for lost baseballs in the field out back and even bringing in chocolate chip cookies to the staff on the third Friday of every month.*

And that was just the half of it.

So when Miss Argyle heard Mr. Tiggle say that the whole school would fall apart without her, she was very flattered.

"Maybe I should take some time off," she said to herself. "It's very peaceful in here." She had a book in one hand that looked interesting. The mouse seemed to have disappeared. There was a pail she could turn upside down for a seat. Another one made a perfect footstool. Mr. Bob, the maintenance man, had the day off. So Miss Argyle switched on the light and spoke to no one but the mops and the brooms.

"For just a little while, I'll rest. I'm sure Mr. Tiggle is wrong. The school wouldn't really fall apart without me, now, would it?"

## Chapter 3
## The Bugaboos Begin

First off, the phones started ringing on all five lines at once, as they usually did at 9:10 each morning. Mr. Tiggle did not know how the phone lines worked when all the lights were blinking at once.

He cut people off.

He started to raise his voice.

His face got as red as licorice.

Before Mr. Tiggle knew it, he had swivelled around three times on Miss Argyle's chair. He wrapped himself inside out and around the cords of the lamp, the computer, and the telephones. And he could not move.

Miss Argyle heard all the phones ringing. For just a minute she felt guilty. Here she was sitting peacefully with dustmops and brooms and enjoying her book. She could hear Mr. Tiggle clearly. He was clearly not speaking clearly.

"Good torning, this is Mr. Miggle. I mean, mood gorning, this is Mupper Illidocket Schelementary Mool."

When Mr. Tiggle was upset or nervous, he stumbled over his syllables like that. He called it making a lipslip. The students called it talking Tiggle-ese.

Miss Argyle couldn't help it. She smiled. She smiled and smiled. "I'll just finish the chapter," she said. "Then I'll go back to my desk." And she read on.

Meanwhile, down in the gym, Mrs. Onyermark was teaching gymnastics to Grade One. Mrs. Onyermark wore a necklace of whistles around her neck and blew them at different times for different reasons.

Two short blasts meant good job.

One long, deep whistle meant try harder.

Three light, high-pitched whistles meant hurry up.

And one short blast meant pay attention!

She blew one short blast.

"And this, class, is the proper way to do a forward roll," she said.

She leaned over and turned the most perfect forward roll you ever saw.

But as she came up in a front tuck position, there was a sound that echoed in the gym.

The sound came from the seat of her pants.

Mrs. Onyermark had ripped the seat right out of her gym suit. The Grade Ones were polite. They tried not to laugh.

Mrs. Onyermark sat there on her bottom and said, "Someone, quickly run down to get Miss Argyle. She has a needle and a thread. Or tell  her please to bring me a sweater to wrap around my ... my ... gluteus maximus."

Mrs. Onyermark always used the proper names for parts of the body. Then she groaned. "And some ice. I think I sprained my ankle."

## Chapter 4
## Trapped

At first, all the Grade Ones stood around and looked at Mrs. Onyermark with concern. But no one offered to go down to the office to get Miss Argyle.

"Who will go for me?" asked Mrs. Onyermark. By this time, most of the class had wandered off.

Some were kicking soccer balls.

Some were bouncing basketballs.

Some were just running up and down the gym chasing each other.

Mrs. Onyermark blew on all her whistles. Only Bobby Andrews listened.

Bobby Andrews was very good at math but often could not join in gym classes because of his asthma.

"I'll go, Mrs. Onyermark," he said. "I'll do it! I'll hurry back as fast as I can."

But Bobby took a wrong turn at the water fountain.

He ended up in the library.

"Bobby," said Mrs. Reed, the librarian, "you poor thing. Is your asthma bothering you again? You come right in and I'll find a good book for us to read."

Bobby went over to her and tugged at her skirt.

"Do you have a needle and thread?" he asked.

"*A Needle and Thread?* I'm not sure I know that book, Bobby."

Mrs. Reed was on a stool reaching for a book. Bobby tugged at her skirt. "No, no, I mean a *real* needle and thread!"

Bobby tugged too hard. Mrs. Reed, the book and the whole book shelf began to wobble.

"Duck!" she yelled at Bobby and threw herself over him.

CRASH! The library shelf toppled over. Mrs. Reed and Bobby were trapped underneath. The shelf made a tent of books above their heads.

"Are you okay, Bobby?" sputtered Mrs. Reed.

"Yes," gasped Bobby. "Are you?"

"I think so." Mrs. Reed gave a little laugh. "Maybe we have just invented a new kind of reading corner. One you can't get out of! Do you think you can crawl through that hole over there?"

Bobby tried. The hole was too small.

"Well," said Mrs. Reed, "we may as well make the best of the situation. Let's read."

She reached above her head and selected a book. It was called *Where the Red Fern Grows*. "One of my favourites," she said. She began reading aloud.

If Miss Argyle had heard that crash, she would have yelled for someone to unlock her and run to the rescue. She was always rescuing people from problems.

She did not hear the crash.

She was fast asleep in the broom closet.

So, by 9:35, while Miss Argyle slept, this was the picture:

Mr. Tiggle was a prisoner in the office.

Mrs. Onyermark was on her mark with a rip in the seat of her pants and a sprained ankle.

Bobby and Mrs. Reed were trapped in a reading tent made out of library shelves.

That was only the beginning of the hullabaloo bugaboo day.

## Chapter 5
## Angela Tarantula

In Grade Four science class, Mr. Potion was conducting an experiment. He was always conducting experiments.

Experiments to find out about electricity and gravity. Experiments with magnets and plants. Then there were experiments on evaporation and vaporization and heat and air.

He loved his work.

"Studying science," Mr. Potion always said, "is really the discovery of the magic in the universe." Sometimes he would create an illusion that made the class ohhh and ahhh. Then he would explain how "the principles of science" were behind the magic.

Mr. Potion's classroom was filled with tubes and jars and bottles. There was usually lots of bubbling going on. There were smells that made everyone's nostrils flare out sideways and tingle.

"What are you making today?" the students were asking.

"You'll see," said Mr. Potion.

That's what he always said. Then he laughed his mysterious mad scientist's laugh.

"That way," he told his wife at night, "my class pays attention. Everyone loves a good mystery."

But on this day, the bubbles started bubbling over the tops of the tubes and jars.

"Quick," instructed Mr. Potion. "Cover your bubbles, class." And so it was that the whole class had each of their hands over each of the jars, and the bubbles kept coming.

Except for Millie Andrews.

"Millie, run down and get the key to my science cupboard from Miss Argyle. I have to add an ingredient that will stop this bubbling."

So Millie left the class and their bubbly troubles behind and hurried down the hall to the office.

No one was there.

Millie did not see Mr. Tiggle who was underneath Miss Argyle's desk. She could not hear him either, for the phones were ringing off the hook and the fax machine was beeping.

Millie went right past the broom closet, and past the library where Bobby and Mrs. Reed were reading quietly.

As she hurried past the gym, she smiled to herself. That Mrs. Onyermark certainly was a good sport. Brave, too. There she was playing monkey-in-the-middle and letting those Grade Ones throw balls over her head.

Then Millie found herself at the door of the Critter Room.

The Critter Room was a whole classroom of creatures that lived at Upper Millidocket Elementary School. Millie loved the Critter Room. She wanted to be a zoologist when she grew up. She already knew a great deal about animals. These were just a few things she knew:

1. *Herbivores* ate plants, *carnivores* ate meat, and *omnivorous* animals ate meats and plants.

2. Chameleons could move their eyes in two directions at once.

3. A cheetah could travel at 116 kilometres per hour.

4. A cockroach could live for ten days without a head.

Millie could not resist. She had a chance to peek into the Critter Room all by herself. She opened the door.

There were three rabbits — Flopsy, Mopsy and Rotten Tail; two gerbils — Goober and Gabber; two snakes — Michael Jordan and

Steffie Graf. Twelve baby chicks were ready to hatch. There were also jars full of cocoons, some fish and salmon eggs in an aquarium and a jar that held a big fat spider called Angela Tarantula. Angela was not really a tarantula but she looked like one.

So Millie went around the room and said, "Hi" to all the critters. At last she came to Angela, her favourite. But Angela was gone.

Disappeared.

## Chapter 6
## Lost Spider, Lost Song

Millie did what any student would do. She began to search for Angela.

Crawling on her hands and knees, she called out softly. "Here, Angela, come on girl." It was the same way she might talk to a dog or a cat. Of course, Angela did not come running to be taken for a walk or be let outdoors to go to the bathroom. But Millie was determined. She would find Angela and return her to her home. Like any good zoologist would.

So this was the picture by 10:00:

Millie was calling to a spider in the Critter Room, while the science room was filling with bubbles.

Bobby and Mrs. Reed were crying at a sad part in the novel, while Mrs. Onyermark was playing a game of dodge ball sitting down.

Mr. Tiggle was on the floor underneath Miss Argyle's desk, as phones rang and faxes beeped.

And Miss Argyle?

She was snoring.

She was having a dream about a desert island where children brought her coconut milk to drink and Mr. Tiggle brought her dinner on a platter.

Meanwhile, down in the music room, a place that was usually full of harmony, the bugaboos continued to turn things upside down even a little more.

"And a one, and a two, and a one, two, three." Mr. Long tapped his baton on the music stand like a real conductor. The class began to play and sing.

"No, no, no!" Mr. Long cried out.

"Start with a bang not a whimper! And remember to breathe, breathe, breathe." He inhaled deeply, made his mouth as round as an o and blew out.

Everyone let out another long sigh. They liked Mr. Long but he was a man who sure could make an entire class start to yawn. Mr. Long Song was his nickname. That's because he made them practice and practice and practice.

"Because practice is what makes a real musician." Besides "breathe, breathe, breathe," this was Mr. Long's favourite expression.

At the moment everyone was trying hard because there was a big music festival coming up in a few weeks.

So Andrea played the recorder.

Simon played the violin.

Tyler beat the bongos.

And the rest of the class sang.

Mr. Long tapped his stick again and said: "All right class, from the top!"

They banged out their beginning and were going along just fine when Mr. Long turned his sheet music and stopped.

"I am missing three pages," he said. "The fifth movement in B flat is missing!"

The class paused, glad for the rest.

"Well, not to worry!"

"Simon, you run and get Miss Argyle to check on the table in the staff room. I'll just dash out to the car and see if I left them in the back seat."

Of course, Simon could not find Miss Argyle in the office. But he knew where the staff room was. When he was younger he thought it was called the laugh room not the staff room because every time the door opened just a crack, he could hear the teachers laughing. Just like ordinary people. He wondered if, at last, he would figure out what was going on in the staff room.

MR. LONG

## Chapter 7
## The Secret of the Staff Room

Simon knocked politely on the staff room door.

He waited.

He opened the door and stepped in.

It was a room with a fridge, a microwave, a coffee machine and dirty coffee cups in the sink.

"Ugh," thought Simon. "Don't they rinse their coffee cups out?

There were two sofas, a round table and several chairs.

The walls were covered with posters and notices.

Simon began to read the posters.

One said: Kids are people, too.

But underneath was a picture of a baboon. Underneath the baboon he read: But they can drive teachers bananas!!!!!

So, thought Simon, that's what they laugh about. Us!

There was another poster. A sunset with a child and an adult holding hands. Simon read: *Students learn best from the teachers who learn from them.*

"Now that's more like it." Simon muttered.

Then he spotted it. A television set. Beside it was a video. He read: "Educational Video Game." Well, that was it.

Simon was hooked on video games. He slipped in the cassette, found the control and flopped down on the couch. Sheet music was the furthest thing from his mind.

As for Mr. Long?  Just as he got to his car, his cellular phone started ringing. He answered.

"Honey?" he said. That was his wife's real name.

"It's time, Herbert. It's time."

Mr. Long went as white as blank sheet music.

"I'll be right home. Breathe," he said into the phone. "Breathe, breathe, breathe,  just like we practiced."

"Whoo, hoo, hoo, grunt," Honey replied.

The Longs were about to have a baby.

Herbert Long roared out of the schoolyard without another thought to sheet music and the fifth movement in B flat.

So ...

In the music room there was a hip hopping sock hop going on while Simon played his video game in the staff room.

Millie was still calling for Angela Tarantula and crawling around on her hands and knees, while Mr. Potion's room was filling with suds.

Bobby and Mrs. Reed were reading  and forgot they were trapped beneath library shelves, while Mrs. Onyermark was being biffed by balls.

Mr. Tiggle was wiggling and jiggling underneath Miss Argyle's desk trying to get free.

And Miss Argyle?

All the while, Miss Argyle slept and smiled. And smiled. And smiled.

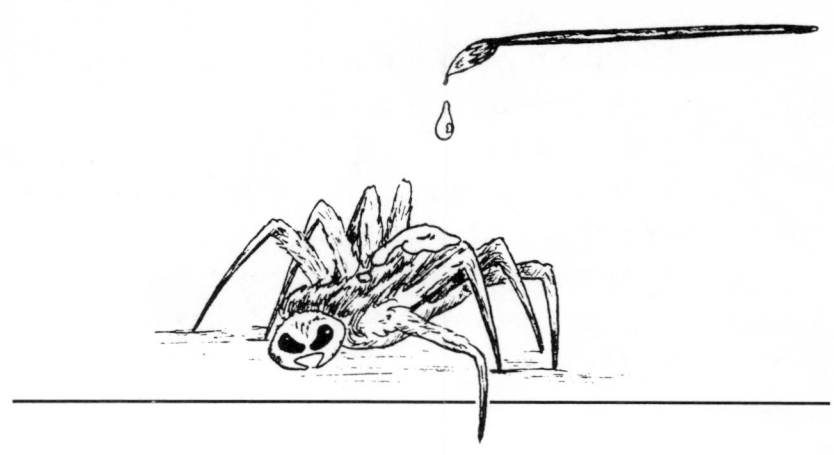

## Chapter 8
## Prissy's Masterpiece

If that wasn't enough of a hullabaloo going on in one place in one day, there was a kerfuffle going on in the Art Room.

The Art Teacher had phoned in sick that morning. Of course, she had not been able to get through on the line. So the Grade Sixes were left unsupervised.

They were fighting among themselves.

Half of the class thought they should go tell someone. The other half were saying, "Why? We're not babies. So like, chill out."

Priscilla Douglas, known as Prissy, was leading the Let's Go Tell group.

Aaron Miller led the Let's Not and Say We Did group.

Aaron blocked the door so Prissy could not get by. He had been doing that all morning.

Finally, Prissy came up with a plan. "Aaron, if you don't let me by, I'll ... I'll —"

"What will you do?" laughed Aaron.

"I'll paint you purple!" she yelled and held out a paint brush dripping with wet paint.

"Go right ahead." Aaron laughed. He knew Prissy would never have the nerve. Prissy Douglas had never done a messy wrong thing in her life.

But to everyone's surprise, Prissy Douglas went wild. She just lost it. "Ballistic" is what they all said afterward.

First, she flicked the brush and splattered purple paint all over Aaron's face and hair. Then when he ducked, she chased him around the room slopping yellow, orange, and green paint along with the purple.

The class started cheering. "Go Prissy, go! Go, Prissy, go!"

"All right ... all right. Stop!" yelled Aaron.

So Prissy stopped.

But by the time she did, the walls and doors were covered with dripping paint.

"Hey cool," said someone. "Look at the designs."

Sure enough, on the walls of the Art Room was a beautiful display of colour and swirls and squiggles.

"So go get someone now, Prissy," laughed Aaron. "You'll be in detention for the rest of your life!"

But Prissy did not seem to hear.

Her eyes were glowing like lasers.

"It felt good," she said. "So good."

Then she dug her hands into wet modelling clay and began throwing that at the walls too. Pretty soon everyone was splattering and chucking and mixing and decorating the room.

Those Grade Sixes left on their own had changed into a wild bunch of mud wrestling, paint splattering twelve-year-olds. They were in wet, sticky trouble.

# Chapter 9
# Max, The Tractor Man

At 11:00 A.M., a man on a small tractor roared into the school yard of Upper Millidocket Elementary School.

The man, whose name was Max, could hear music and the squeals of children.

He could hear balls bouncing and ringing telephones.

"Ah ... school days," he smiled to himself. "So much different than when I was kid."

Max read over his orders.

> Tear down shed at back of school.
> Go to office and ask for Miss Argyle,
>   the secretary, before you start.

But Max, the tractor man, could not find Miss Argyle in the office.

So he shrugged and got back onto his tractor and drove around to the back of the school.

"There's the shed," he said to himself. "No problem. I can have that down in less than half an hour."

This shed was attached to the back of the school. In fact, it was really part of the school building. Max did not see the other shed at the far end of the baseball field.

The shed he was supposed to destroy.

So he backed up his tractor and began his work.

**RUMMMMMBLE!**

Upper Millidocket Elementary School WAS ABOUT TO FALL APART.

Inside the school, everyone stopped what they were doing. It was like the whole school stopped breathing.

Earthquake! is what they thought.

**RUMMMMMBLE!**

Miss Argyle woke up and blinked.

**RUMMMMMBLE!**

She looked at her watch.

She knew exactly what was happening.

With the strength of 62 elephants and 43 rhinos she broke open the broom closet door.

She ran out the door, around to the back of the school. If Max pulled down the wall he was working on, part of the school might crash down with it.

"STOP!!!!!!!!!!" screamed Miss Argyle. "Or this whole school will fall apart!"

Max nearly fell off his tractor. He did not know what was happening. A woman with red hair flying every which way had jumped in front of his tractor. She began waving her arms up and down. He slammed on his brakes.

Miss Argyle ran up to him and explained quickly. "That shed, not this one!"

"Oops!" said Max. "I'll see if I can repair the damage at once."

"Please do," said Miss Argyle in her very best secretary voice.

Inside the school, once everyone realized there were no more rumbles and no earthquake about to happen, they continued with their fun.

So, when Miss Argyle ran back into the school, guess what she discovered?

First, she heard yelling and screaming coming from the Art Room.

She burst through the door like a sneeze.

"Prissy Douglas!"

Miss Argyle's voice cut through all the hullabaloo like a buzz-saw.

The Grade Sixes stopped instantly.

"I will give you thirty minutes. Start cleaning — all of you!" said Miss Argyle. "When

I return I want everything and everyone to be clean, clean, clean ...!"

The Grade Sixes had never heard Miss Argyle so angry.

"Sure Miss Argyle. We'll take care of it," squeaked Aaron. Miss Argyle was his mother's second cousin.

Miss Argyle followed her ears to the music room. It sounded like a rap concert was going on.

"And what is happening in here?"

Grade Fours explained that Simon went looking for sheet music and the last they saw of Mr. Long was his red Volkswagen squealing out of the parking lot.

"Sit down in your seats and begin your math homework," she said.

"Math in music class?" whined Tyler.

Miss Argyle simply raised one eyebrow and put on Beethoven.

Harmony was restored to the music room once more.

But Miss Argyle had a feeling that this was only the beginning of her troubles. She could feel bugaboos all around her.

Where, oh where was Mr. Tiggle?

# Chapter 10
## Spiders and Snakes

Miss Argyle went directly to the staff room. This was the time of day when Mr. Tiggle liked to have a second cup of coffee.

There was Simon. His eyes were like marbles as he stared at the TV screen.

"Simon." No answer.

"Simon." No answer.

"Simon!" Still no answer. Not even a blink of his marble eyes.

Simon, like some kind of robot, stared straight ahead.

Miss Argyle went and switched off the television set.

Simon jumped up.

"Aw, Mom, just five more minutes."

"Simon!" Miss Argyle snapped her fingers. "I am not your mother. You are not at home.

This is school, and what are you doing in the staff room?"

Simon's eyes changed from marbles to eyes again. Then they grew to the size of tennis balls. He blinked back to reality. "Um ... just looking for —"

"These perhaps?" said Miss Argyle. She grabbed three pieces of paper off the table. "Return to the music room and do your math."

"Math in music class?" he whined.

"And I won't tell anyone you were playing video games in the staff room."

Simon gulped. He did as he was told.

He had never known that Miss Argyle could be so bossy.

What next? thought Miss Argyle.

Next she heard something strange.

"Angela, Angela, come on girl. Come out, come out, wherever you are!"

A voice was coming from the Critter Room.

Miss Argyle opened the door slowly.

Millie hopped up and told Miss Argyle about Angela.

Miss Argyle smiled. This was a minor problem.

"Now think, Millie, if you were a spider, where would you go?"

Millie scratched her head.

"Okay, let me put it another way. If you were spider what would you do?"

Millie snapped her fingers. "Spin a web?"

"Right. And what would you need to spin a web?"

"Some place to hang my web from. Like a corner."

Sure enough, high in the corner of the Critter Room was a beautiful web and Angela was happily spinning away in the middle of it.

"Shall we leave her there instead of putting her back in her bottle?" suggested Miss Argyle.

"Yes, it is best for animals to remain in their natural habitat," said Millie.

"Perhaps we should let the snakes go as well," said Miss Argyle.

And they did. They watched as Michael Jordan and Steffie Graf slithered happily out the window and raced to the basketball and tennis courts.

Millie suggested they keep the rabbits because they had been in the school since they were babies and probably wouldn't know what to do in the wild. Miss Argyle thought that was a wise decision.

"Now Millie, what are you doing here, anyhow?"

Millie shrieked and covered her mouth with her hands.

"Ahhh! Mr. Potion! He needs the key to his science cupboard!"

Miss Argyle had many keys on a bracelet around her arm.

Millie started hopping up and down.

"They're in trouble down there."

"What kind of trouble, Millie?" Miss Argyle imagined the worst.

Millie's voice was just a croak. "Bubble trouble."

## Chapter 11
## The Clean Class & Off yer Mark

By the time Millie and Miss Argyle reached the science room, suds were slipping out from underneath the door.

The entire class was covered with foam. They were, without a doubt, the cleanest class in the world at that moment.

"Mr. Potion, what ARE you trying to do?'

"Making bubbles?" He sounded like he was gargling.

"Well, it seems your experiment was a great success."

Miss Argyle waded through the suds and unlocked the science cupboard.

"And what do you need?"

"Salt," gargled Mr. Potion. "Just start sprinkling salt on bubbles and you will see that the chemical reaction of the sodium will reduce the effervescence."

"I'll leave you to it," said Miss Argyle. Millie started shaking the salt over the jars and tubes and the bottles. Everyone started shouting, "Quick! Pass the salt!"

That's when Miss Argyle heard what sounded like thunder above her head. It was coming from the gym. She ran up the stairs, two at a time.

"What took you so long?" yelled Mrs. Onyermark. "My pants are ripped and my ankle is throbbing. I sent Bobby to get you an hour ago."

"Bobby? My heavens, here." Miss Argyle wrapped her sweater around Mrs. Onyermark's waist.

"Grade One, Grade One ... sit down and pretend you are rocks. Silent rocks." They did as they were told. They had never seen Miss Argyle look like a wild woman.

"I'll help you to the nurse's office," Miss Argyle said to Mrs. Onyermark. Then Miss Argyle propped Mrs. Onyermark against her shoulder.

As they hobbled past the library, Miss Argyle spotted the upset shelf. She left Mrs. Onyermark on a seat in the hall.

"Hello? Mrs. Reed?" hollered Miss Argyle.

"Yoohoo. We're under here."

Miss Argyle got down on her hands and knees and peeked underneath the shelf. There sat Bobby and Mrs. Reed. They were both hunched over but looking just as cosy as if they were sitting around a campfire telling stories.

"Are you okay?" asked Miss Argyle. She was sure she saw tears in their eyes.

"We're just fine. This book is quite sad at times," sniffed Mrs. Reed. "In fact we've read seven chapters."

"Can you get us out?" asked Bobbie. He didn't think he could take Mrs. Reed's crying much longer.

Maybe it was the excitement. Maybe it was the adrenalin.

Whatever it was, Miss Argyle found some sort of superhero strength.

She grunted and groaned.

She heaved and huffed.

She made the opening big enough for Bobbie and Miss Reed to crawl through.

Bobbie came out first. He was impressed.

"You lift weights or something?" he said.

But Miss Argyle did not hear him. "Please help Mrs. Onyermark to the nurse's office."

Then Miss Argyle, with as much courage as she had, headed towards the main office. Something was wrong, really wrong. Where was Mr. Tiggle in all of this hullabaloo?

## Chapter 12
## Tiggle Trouble

When Miss Argyle entered the office, she noticed how many things were bleeping and blinking.

Then she spotted one of Mr. Tiggle's shoes.

It was in the wastepaper basket.

Then she saw the tip of the other shoe underneath her desk.

There was Mr. Tiggle, lying face down, not moving.

"Heavens, he's dead," she thought.

But Mr. Tiggle, tired from so much struggling, had fallen asleep.

Carefully, she unwound the cords from around Mr. Tiggle and put everything back in place.

Then she woke Mr. Tiggle by whispering softly in his ear.

"Mr. Tiggle?"

He blinked his eyes open slowly.

"Miss Argyle! I thought I'd lost you forever. I had the strangest dream. I, I dreamt that this whole school almost fell apart because ... because I ... I couldn't find you!"

"There, there Mr. Tiggle. It was just a bad dream."

Then Mr. Tiggle sat up. His forehead wrinkled like an accordion.

"But where, in the name of Upper Millidocket Elementary School, where were you all morning?"

Just then the phone rang. Mr. Long was on the line. He was so happy he almost sang what he had to say.

"Miss Argyle. We had a baby girl. We will name her Sonata. Tell everyone for me. And ... I almost forgot ... I left my music class!"

"Not to worry," said Miss Argyle. "Congratulations! I'm sure you'd like to talk to Mr. Tiggle."

By the time the lunch-time bell rang, things were almost normal.

Except that the bugaboo feeling stayed in the air.

All afternoon, as Mr. Tiggle went around the school, he discovered many things. One of the things he discovered was Mrs. Day, the resource teacher. She had gone to Miss Argyle to get a poster laminated, and she had laminated her scarf instead.

"How do you unlaminate a teacher, Miss Argyle?" said Mr. Tiggle scowling.

Miss Argyle couldn't help it. It must have been the stress of everything. She started laughing and she could not stop.

Miss Day, stiff as a board, tried to look insulted. "Be brave," gasped Miss Argyle between her giggles. "Try to keep a stiff upper lip, now! Get it?" Then she laughed so hard she had to excuse herself to get a drink of water.

Mr. Tiggle was still scowling at her as she packed her desk up neatly at the end of the day.

He spoke in a very serious manner.

"Miss Argyle, tomorrow morning, after the announcements, I should like to see you in my office. As a result of your actions, today was not another wonderful Upper Millidocket Elementary School Day. It was a hullabaloo bugaboo day. We must talk."

Miss Argyle nodded. Never in twenty years had she been asked to go to the principal's office.

She took the long way home that night. She walked for an hour in the park, then sat on a bench to watch the pigeons. Whatever had possessed her to stay in the broom closet? What had she been thinking? The school really did depend on her. Mr. Tiggle was right. All because of her, it had turned into a hullabaloo bugaboo day.

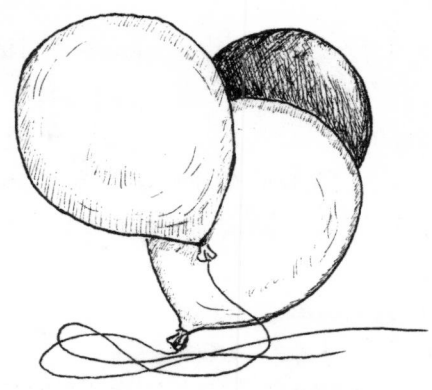

# Chapter 13
# The Firing Squad

Miss Argyle lived in a small one-bedroom house. There was a large backyard garden where she went to sit and relax. That night, after she lovingly tended her roses, she sat in the garden with her cup of tea. Ophelia, her cat, sat beside her. They both listened to the radio. The only other sound was the click of Miss Argyle's needles as she finished the sweater she was making for Mr. Long's baby.

Miss Argyle had a sadness in the middle of her stomach that felt like a twisted ball of yarn. She knew that tomorrow Mr. Tiggle would say: "Perhaps it is time for you to leave. I am sorry, but you are fired!"

"I have had the best job in the world," she said out loud to Ophelia. "I have lived among children, and teachers who love children. They have kept me laughing and kept me young. I have been part of a very exceptional school. Besides you, Ophelia, they are my family."

Ophelia purred and rubbed up against Miss Argyle's leg.

She did not sleep well that night. Part of the reason was that her sadness hung upon her like a wet soggy blanket. The other reason is that she had slept a great deal that day in the broom closet.

When she did sleep, she had a nightmare. Everyone was in front of her. Bobby and Mrs. Reed, Mr. Tiggle, Millie and Simon, Mr. Long and Mr. Potion, Mrs. Onyermark and Prissy Douglas and especially Miss Day. They had her up against the wall of the shed.

"We are the firing squad!" they yelled together.

"One, two, three! You're fired!!!!!"

Miss Argyle woke up and made herself another cup of tea. She watched the clock until it was time to get ready for work.

When she arrived at the school that morning, it seemed like no one would look her in the eye. In the staff room, no one was laughing.

She was sure Mr Tiggle's poem during the announcements was meant just for her. The poem went like this:

*Some days are happy, some hullabaloo.*
*Yesterday we had the bugaboos.*
*Today will be different and our school will be*
*The exceptional school that we know it can be!!!!*

"Now," he said, "Miss Argyle, please come with me."

Miss Argyle guessed he was about to show her the damage done in the Art Room or the soggy mess of the science room or the missing snakes in the Critter Room. He probably wanted to charge her for the damage she had done before firing her.

He opened the gym doors.

"Surprise! Surprise!"

The entire school was there.

"Three cheers for Miss Argyle!!!!"

"We love you Miss Argyle!!!!!"

"There has never been a secretary like our Miss Argyle!!!!!"

Signs and streamers decorated the gym. Parents were there. Everyone was clapping.

Max, the tractor man, stepped out of the crowd. He was clapping louder than anyone. "The woman who saved the school from falling apart," he said.

Max whispered in her ear. "I couldn't help it, I had to tell your boss what a brave thing you did to save this school."

By this time Miss Argyle was dabbing at her eyes.

Mr. Tiggle made a speech. He hardly made any lipslips. Except for the time he introduced Max.

First he said, "This is Tax, the Mactor Man."

Then he said, "I mean this is Trax, the Muctor Man."

Finally he said, "I mean this is MAX the Tractor Man.

But mostly he talked about Miss Argyle.

He talked about how a person like Miss Argyle is so valuable to a school. He gave her a bouquet of flowers. Pink roses. Her favourite.

"Secretary's Day should be every day," he said. Miss Argyle was speechless. Finally, she laughed.

"Mr. Tiggle, please remember to say your poem every day from now on. After all, a poem a day keeps the bugaboos away!" shouted everyone all together.

"I will," promised Mr. Tiggle. And he never forgot again.

Well, almost never.

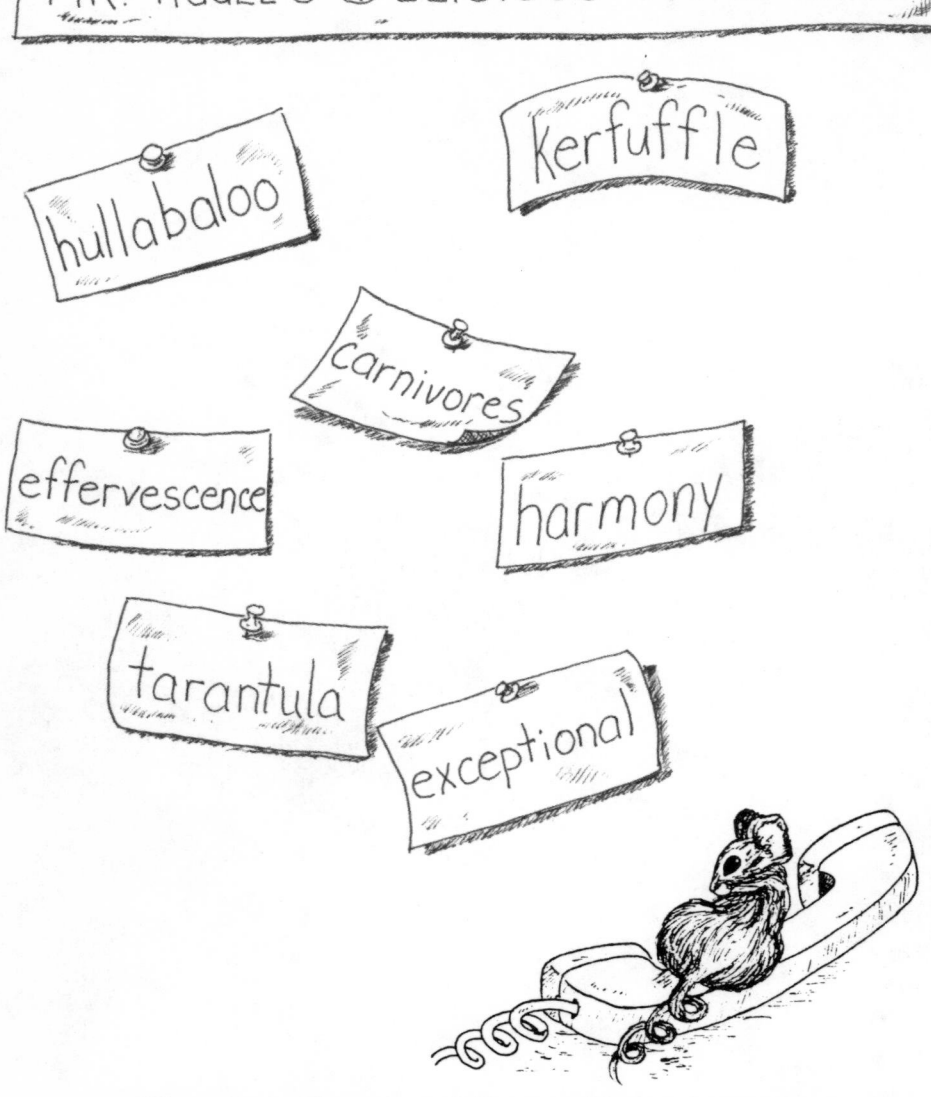

MR. TIGGLE'S DELICIOUS WORD LIST

hullabaloo

Kerfuffle

carnivores

effervescence

harmony

tarantula

exceptional

Watch for further Sheree Fitch adventures (and misadventures) at Upper Millidocket Elementary School.